This Ladybird Book belongs to:

_____

_____

_____

_____

Retold by Audrey Daly
Illustrated by Martin Salisbury

Cover illustration by Walter Porter

Copyright © Ladybird Books USA 1996

Originally published in the United Kingdom by Ladybird Books Ltd © 1993

First American edition by Ladybird Books USA
An Imprint of Penguin USA Inc.
375 Hudson Street, New York, New York 10014

Printed in Great Britain
10 9 8 7 6 5 4 3 2 1

ISBN 0-7214-5621-9

FAVORITE TALES

Jack and the Beanstalk

nce upon a time there was a poor boy named Jack who lived with his mother. All they had in the world was one cow.

One day Jack's mother said, "We have no money for food. We shall have to sell the cow."

So Jack took the cow to market.
On the way, he met a man.

"If you give me your cow," said the man,
"I will give you some magic beans that
are far better than money."

The magic beans looked wonderful, so Jack gave the man the cow. Then he ran home as fast as he could.

"How much money did you get for the cow?" asked his mother.

"I got something much better than money," said Jack, showing her the magic beans.

"You were tricked! These beans are worthless!" cried his mother angrily. "We can't even eat them." With that, she threw them out the window.

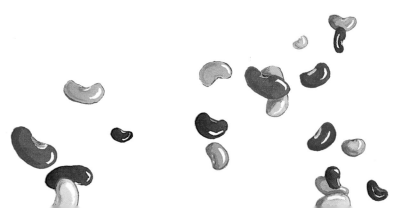

When Jack woke up the next morning, his window was covered with green leaves. Overnight, a huge beanstalk had grown in the very spot his mother had thrown the magic beans. The beanstalk was so tall it reached up to the clouds.

"I must find out what's at the top," Jack said. And he began to climb the beanstalk.

Up and up he climbed. At last he found himself in a bare, rocky wilderness.

There wasn't a tree or an animal to be seen, just a long road stretching into the distance. Jack decided to follow it.

By evening he came to the gate of an enormous castle. Tired and hungry, Jack knocked loudly on the large door.

"Could you please give me some food and a bed for the night?" Jack asked the woman who answered.

"Oh no," said the woman. "My husband is a fierce giant who hates strangers." But Jack looked so hungry that she took pity on him and gave him supper.

Just as Jack was enjoying some hot soup, the castle began to shake. "My husband is coming!" cried the woman. Then she quickly hid Jack in a cupboard.

The giant stomped in and roared,

"Fee, fie, foe, fum,
I smell the blood of an Englishman!
Be he alive or be he dead,
I'll grind his bones to make my bread!"

"Nonsense!" said his wife. "There is no one here." And she gave the giant his supper.

When he had finished his supper, the giant boomed, "Bring me my hen!"

His wife brought a little hen and put it on the table.

"Lay!" shouted the giant.

Jack peeked out from his hiding place. To
his amazement, every time the giant
shouted, the hen laid a little golden egg.

When he had twelve golden eggs, the giant
fell asleep.

As soon as it was quiet, Jack crept out of the cupboard and grabbed the little hen. Then, careful not to wake the giant, Jack tiptoed out of the castle.

He ran and ran until he was back at the top of the beanstalk. Quickly, he climbed down and took the magic hen to his mother.

How pleased she was! "Long ago a wicked giant stole this hen from your father," she said. "Now that we have her back, we will never be poor again!"

Jack lived happily with his mother for a while. But he longed for another adventure, so one day he decided to climb up the beanstalk again.

Just as before, Jack reached the castle toward evening. And once again the giant's wife hid him when they heard the giant roar,

"Fee, fie, foe, fum,
I smell the blood of an Englishman!
Be he alive or be he dead,
I'll grind his bones to make my bread!"

After supper the giant shouted, "Fetch me my money bags!" His wife brought him four sacks filled with gold coins.

The giant emptied the sacks onto the table and counted the coins over and over again. At last he put the money back in the sacks and fell asleep.

Quick as a flash, Jack took the gold coins and ran all the way home.

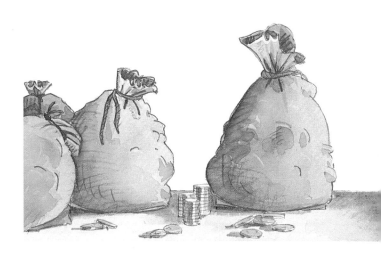

His mother was delighted when she saw the money bags. "The giant stole this money from your father," she said. "You have done well to bring it back."

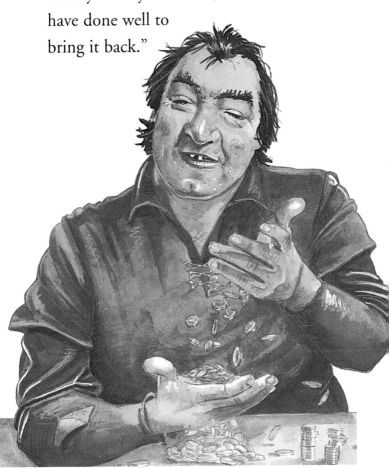

Jack and his mother were now quite rich. But Jack still was not satisfied. He wanted to try to trick the giant one last time. So back up the magic beanstalk he climbed.

This time the giant asked his wife for
his beautiful golden harp. "Play!" roared
the giant, and the harp began to play
soft music.

The music was so sweet and gentle that it
sent the giant to sleep. But when Jack
crept out and seized it, the harp cried out,
"Master! Master!"

The giant woke up in a rage, just in time to see Jack disappearing through the door with the harp. "Stop, thief!" the giant roared as he ran after Jack.

Jack ran for his life. The giant took huge strides and reached out his large hand to grab Jack. But Jack slipped through his fingers and scrambled down the beanstalk, shouting, "Mother! Mother! Bring the ax!"

Jack grabbed the ax with both hands and struck a mighty blow to the beanstalk. *Thwack!* The beanstalk toppled to the ground, and the giant tumbled down with an earthshaking thud.

That was the end of the giant. Jack and
his mother were never poor again.

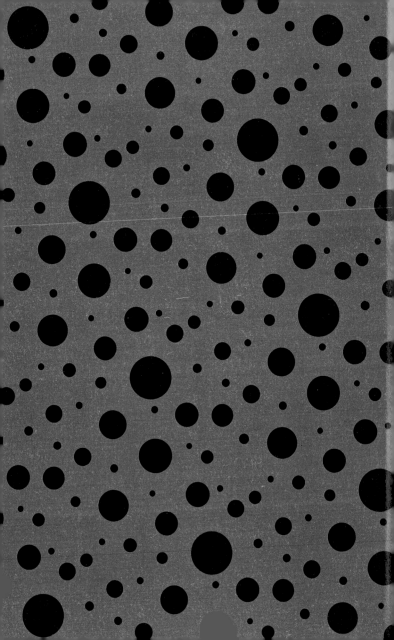